GOOD BUDDY

written by Michael Burgan
illustrated by Stephanie Milanowski

**McGraw-Hill
School Division**

New York   Farmington

Roy Allen squirmed restlessly in the high-backed kitchen chair. Behind him, his mother was working with a pair of clippers, attempting to give Roy a haircut.

"Do I *have* to go?" Roy asked in a high-pitched, whiny voice.

"Hold still," his mother scolded, "I almost trimmed your right ear! Yes, you have to go," she said emphatically.

"I hate that place," Roy said. "It smells like antiseptic and medicine, and there's nothing for me to do there. It's so boring!"

"You don't go to a nursing home to have fun," Mrs. Allen countered. "You go to see your grandfather. Don't you like visiting him?"

Roy lowered his head, feeling somewhat ashamed. "Sure I do—I love Grandpa, but that place..."

Roy remembered the last time he had gone, when all of his grandfather's friends had gathered around him. They asked the same questions they had asked on previous visits. How was he doing in school, what games did he play, what teams did he root for? Then some of the ladies pulled on his cheeks and commented on how cute he was. After five or six pulls, his face turned crimson and it really hurt.

Roy's mother had taught him to always be polite, though, and Roy knew some of the people in the nursing home didn't have family to visit them. Understandably, conversations with Roy and his family cheered them up a little.

"Would it be any easier to go if you brought a friend along?" Mrs. Allen inquired slyly.

"A friend?" Roy repeated. "Who would want to come with me to a nursing home?"

"I'll bet Buddy would love to go with us," Mrs. Allen replied.

"Buddy!" Roy exclaimed. "How can I bring a dog into the nursing home?"

Roy looked over at his golden retriever, and, as if on cue, Buddy raised his head and began to thump his tail enthusiastically against the carpet. Roy fed Buddy and walked him . . . well, *some* of the time. His mom took Buddy to the veterinarian for his regular checkups, but Roy knew Buddy loved him best. Well, to be truthful, Buddy loved him and Grandpa best.

As she put down her clippers, Mrs. Allen began to reply to Roy's question. "The nursing home just started a new program called Pet Therapy. Now people can bring their pets with them when they visit their relatives," Mrs. Allen explained. "Most folks in nursing homes are pleased to have animals around and, in fact, doctors are discovering that pets make sick or lonely people feel better. Maybe bringing Buddy will help cheer you up, too."

"I guess it would be fun to bring him along," Roy agreed.

"I have to run a few quick errands," Mrs. Allen said over her shoulder. "Stay with Grandma and, when I get back, we'll all leave for the nursing home."

"Okay, Mom," Roy replied, watching her go.

"Want to go for a ride in the car, Buddy?" asked Roy.

Buddy ran over to Roy, wagging his tail and barking with excitement.

"We're going to see Grandpa!" Roy explained, as he petted the retriever's head. For the first time, he was actually excited about going to the nursing home.

An hour later, Roy, his mom, his grandma, and Buddy were cruising up the long, winding driveway of the nursing home. When Roy opened the car door, Buddy jumped out. After smelling the air, Buddy sauntered up to an elderly woman on the sidewalk. She was petite, with gray hair, and she steadied her steps carefully with a cane. When the woman saw Buddy, however, she stopped and smiled from ear to ear.

"Be careful, Buddy," Roy admonished. "Don't bother the lady."

"Oh, nonsense, he's not a bother at all," the woman said. "I love dogs, and I haven't seen many since I've been here." She gingerly bent down and stroked Buddy's head.

"Come on, Buddy," Mrs. Allen called. "Time to go inside."

They stopped at the front office first to greet Mrs. Simon, who worked there as a receptionist.

"I see you've got a friend with you today, Roy," Mrs. Simon observed. "What a beautiful dog! Is he yours?"

"Yes," Roy answered, "his name's Buddy, and we're taking him to see my grandfather."

"He's in the living room," Mrs. Simon informed them. Then she turned to Mrs. Allen and asked, "Do you have a copy of Buddy's medical records?"

"I picked them up this morning," Mrs. Allen answered, handing over a copy of Buddy's vaccination card.

"Thank you," said Mrs. Simon. Then she took a sheet of paper from her desk drawer and placed it in the printer. After typing Buddy's name on her computer keyboard, she printed the page out. "See, it's official," she said, handing Roy a certificate that said Buddy was a "Pet Therapist" at the nursing home.

After saying good-bye to Mrs. Simon, Roy and Buddy followed Mrs. Allen and her mother down a brightly painted corridor decorated with prints of famous landscapes. Then they entered the large living room.

A television played in one corner of the sun-drenched room, and, although a few people seemed to be enjoying the program, others looked rather bored. Still other residents were reading or looking out of the windows.

Roy shuffled his feet, starting to feel uncomfortable. Just then, Buddy gave a friendly *woof* and headed toward the left side of the room, as far as the leash would take him.

Sure enough, there was Grandpa, sitting in his wheelchair and staring out a window. Roy felt a sudden twinge of sadness.

"Hello, Dad," Mrs. Allen called, as they approached him. "How are you doing today?"

Mr. Nemeth looked up as his wife bent down to kiss him.

"Hi, Grandpa," Roy said, giving him a big hug, "look who's here to see you!"

Mr. Nemeth appreciated his family's visit, but he was flabbergasted to see Buddy. "Buddy!" he cried, opening his eyes as wide as he could, "what are you doing here, fella? I haven't seen you in ages."

A huge grin spread across the old man's face as he petted the gentle dog, whose squirming betrayed the effort of his self-control. Buddy would have loved to jump up on his old friend, but he had to be content with licking his hand.

"Atta boy," Grandpa said, as Buddy began to calm down. Grandpa rubbed under the large dog's chin, and Buddy thumped his tail excitedly on the sparkling tiled floor.

Roy was relieved to see his grandfather's face so filled with joy. Roy never knew what kind of mood Grandpa would be in when they came to visit. Sometimes he sat and didn't say much at all, but, with Buddy there, Grandpa was full of enthusiasm.

Then a disturbing thought flickered across his mind and Grandpa turned to his wife and asked, "Now, Martha, did you get permission to bring Buddy in here? I don't want to get into any trouble with the management, or the staff."

"Of course we did, dear. Roy, show your grandfather what you got from the office," Mrs. Nemeth said, giving Roy a wink.

9

By the time Roy's grandfather looked up from the certificate with a big grin, quite a number of the residents had gathered around to see the new pet therapist.

"What a cutie," one woman exclaimed.

"I once had a golden retriever that resembled this one—called him Cody," an older gentleman with a hearing aid confided to Roy. "Good animal he was. Gentle as they come."

"Look at him sniffing the air," a woman observed. "They do that out of instinct. Those retrievers are great sniffers."

"And a loyal dog to have hunting with you, too," a man next to Mrs. Nemeth added. Then he began telling her about the time his dog went duck hunting with him and warned him about a dangerous snake called a water mocassin.

All this time, Buddy sat there quietly, while excitedly wagging his tail. And, when people started coming over to him to pet him and praise him, he was as good as gold. "Gentle as they come," the man with the hearing aid said again, this time clearly referring to Buddy.

Just then, a nurse entered the living room and, upon seeing the hubbub of activity surrounding Roy's grandfather, she asked with a smile, "And what's going on in here, Mr. Nemeth?"

"My grandson brought his dog, Buddy," said Grandpa, pointing at the center of attention. "It's all right that he's here, isn't it?"

"Sure, Mr. Nemeth, lots of hospitals and nursing homes are encouraging visitors to bring their pets onto the premises. Some nursing homes even keep their own pets for the residents to care for."

"That's a switch," Roy's grandfather said. "We take care of someone, instead of someone taking care of us."

"Besides making them happy, what else can the pets do for senior citizens?" Roy asked.

"Well," the nurse began, "have you ever heard of high blood pressure?"

Roy knew a lot about it, so he confidently replied, "My Grandpa has high blood pressure, but he takes pills for it. If it's not treated, though, people can have heart attacks or even strokes."

The nurse nodded and then continued, "Well, doctors say that having a pet around can help lower someone's blood pressure."

"And besides that," Grandpa said, "having Buddy around just makes me plain happy."

The nurse nodded again, and said, "A friendly dog or cat can make sick people feel happier, and when people are happy, their bodies become stronger. Then they can fight illnesses better."

"What do you think of that, Buddy?" Roy said. "You're almost as important as a doctor."

"He's certainly improved the disposition of everyone in this room," Mrs. Allen commented. "What a fantastic way to brighten someone's day!"

More residents were now coming into the living room, for the news about Buddy had spread and everyone wanted to see him. They petted him and cooed softly to him. Others, a bit more timid, stood on the edge of the circle, relating stories about the pets that they had had. Some even recalled the pets they had when they were no older than Roy.

"This is wonderful," the nurse whispered to Mrs. Allen before leaving the living room. "Thank you so much for signing Buddy up for the Pet Therapy Program."

One woman approached Roy and asked, "Can your dog perform any tricks?"

"He can sit up and beg," Roy said. "And he's great at playing fetch."

"Maybe he'll fetch this ball," the woman said, pulling an old tennis ball out of the pocket of her cardigan sweater and handing it to Roy. "I found it out on the lawn during my morning walk."

Roy whistled for Buddy to follow him outside through the sliding glass door and the big golden retriever was happy to oblige. Then Roy threw the ball and Buddy went bounding across the lawn and scampering around a maple tree to disappear behind a forsythia bush. Then, with his head held high, Buddy rounded the opposite side of the bush with the tennis ball in his mouth. Everyone in the room cheered, and they were still clapping when the dog dropped the ball at Roy's feet.

By this time, several of the residents had
ventured outside to watch. The next time Roy threw
the ball, Buddy retrieved it and dropped it at the feet
of the woman who had found it on the lawn. People
began to chuckle and giggle. They were enchanted by
this loving, four-legged visitor. Eventually, Buddy had
involved almost half the circle in the game.

"I've never had this much fun here before,"
Grandpa said, trying to stifle his laughter.

The old gentleman with the hearing aid was
about to throw the ball again when a blaring siren
was heard. The group turned to see an ambulance
come round the circular drive and pull to a stop.

"Aaaoooh," Buddy began to howl.

One of the women leaned forward to cover
Buddy's ears with her hands. Then they all decided
to go back inside.

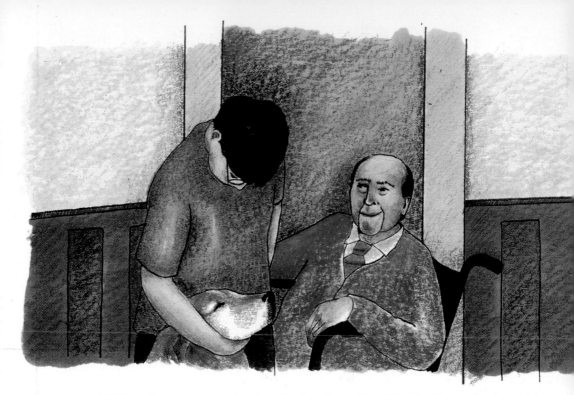

"Thanks so much for bringing Buddy," Grandpa said, patting his grandson on the back. "He's made us all feel one hundred years younger, and happier, too!" Then he added, "I want you to promise me something, Roy."

"What, Grandpa?" Roy inquired.

"Promise me that you'll bring Buddy every time you come."

"It's a deal," Roy said. "From now on, Buddy comes whenever I do—and I think I'll be coming more often, too. How does Thursday sound?"

"Thursday," repeated some of the residents, as if they were attempting to memorize it.

"Thursday sounds great to me," agreed Mrs. Allen with a big grin—and Buddy ran up to her, as if on cue, for a belly scratching.

"Looks like you got the job, Buddy!" commented Roy. "*Now* it's official."